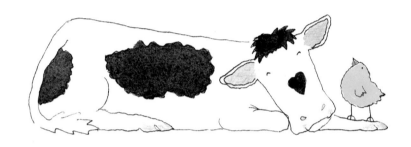

Little Cow

First published in the UK in 1998 by
 Belitha Press Limited, London House,
Great Eastern Wharf, Parkgate Road,
London SW11 4NQ.

ISBN 1 85561 801 X

British Library Cataloguing in Publication Data
for this book is available from the British Library

Printed in Belgium

Editor: Honor Head
Designer: Helen James
Calligraphy: Jan Barger

Little Cow

Jan Barger

Belitha Press

Mama Cow and Little Cow were resting in the afternoon sun.

'Move, Cow!' said the farmer.
'I can't get my tractor past you.'

'Moo,' said Mama.
'Little Cow is sleeping.'

'Move, Cow!' said Horse.
'You're in the way.'

'Moo,' said Mama.
'Little Cow is sleeping.'

'Move, Cow!' said Donkey. 'I've got
to meet some children for a ride.'

'Moo,' said Mama.
'Little Cow is sleeping.'

'Move, Cow!' said Pig.
'I want to get to my mud puddle.'

'Moo,' said Mama.
'Little Cow is sleeping.'

'Move, Cow!' said Sheep.
'I need to find my flock.

'Moo,' said Mama.
'Little Cow is sleeping.'

'Move, Cow!' said Tortoise.
'I'm in a hurry.'

'Moo,' said Mama.
'Little Cow is sleeping.'

'Move, Cow!' said Hen.
'My chicks have scattered.'

'Moo,' said Mama.
'Little Cow is sleeping.'

'Please move, Cow,' said the farmer's wife. 'It's feeding time.'

So Mama Cow took Little Cow
home for supper.

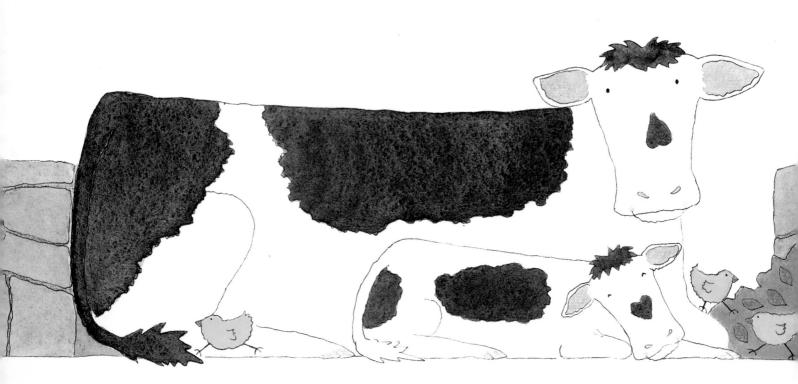